TREASURY
of
CHRISTMAS
TALES

pi
kids ®

publications international, ltd.

Contributing Writer
Carolyn Quattrocki

Cover Illustrations
Wayne Parmenter and Sally Schaedler

Illustrations
Susan Spellman

"A Christmas Carol" is adapted from *A Christmas Carol* by Charles Dickens.

"The Littlest Angel" is adapted from the story of the same name by Sister Maryanna, O.P.

"'Twas the Night Before Christmas" was written by Clement Moore.

Louis Weber, C.E.O.
Publications International, Ltd.
7373 North Cicero Avenue
Lincolnwood, Illinois 60712

Ground Floor, 59 Gloucester Place, London W1U 8JJ

Permission is never granted for commercial purposes.

Customer Service: 1-800-595-8484 or customer_service@pilbooks.com

www.pilbooks.com

p i kids is a trademark of Publications International, Ltd., and is registered in the United States.

Manufactured in China.

8 7 6 5 4 3 2 1

ISBN-13: 978-1-4127-8375-0
ISBN-10: 1-4127-8375-5

Contents

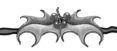

A Christmas

CAROL

The day was Christmas Eve, many years ago. The weather was cold and snowy. Busy in his countinghouse, old Ebenezer Scrooge was counting his money. In the freezing outer office, Bob Cratchit, Scrooge's clerk, sat shivering.

"Tomorrow is Christmas Day," said Bob Cratchit meekly to his employer. "Will you be needing me to come to work, sir?"

"Christmas Day? Bah, humbug!" replied Scrooge. "I suppose you must have the day off, but be sure you are here even earlier the day after. Christmas is a poor excuse for being a lazy clerk!"

*J*ust then, Scrooge looked up with a frown from his counting desk, having heard a sound outside the window of his office. He went to look.

Carolers had gathered in the street, and Scrooge could hear their cheerful song:

"God rest ye merry gentlemen!
Let nothing you dismay!"

Scrooge threw open the window and shouted to the carolers, "Be on your way! Can't you see we are working here?"

"Merry Christmas!" the carolers sang out.

Before he closed the window, Scrooge replied, "Bah, humbug! Only fools go around with 'Merry Christmas' on their lips!"

Scrooge went back to counting his money. A smile came to his face as he looked at the piles of gold coins on the table.

He was interrupted by a knock at his door. Two gentlemen came into his office. The first said, "We are here to collect some money for the poor. This is Christmas Eve, and many have no food for the holidays."

Scrooge remarked, "I haven't time for all this talk of Christmas. What rubbish! Let the poor take care of themselves. Don't bother me."

"But, sir," protested the second man, "surely you must want to help those in need."

Shaking his fist, Scrooge croaked, "Christmas— bah, humbug!"

That night, Scrooge went home to his lonely house. He ate a cold supper, then went to bed.

In the middle of the night, he was awakened suddenly by a strange noise in his room. He sat up in his bed and stared at the ghostly figure in front of him. He saw what looked like a person in a white robe moving slowly toward his bed.

The figure spoke to Scrooge: "Come with me. I am the Ghost of Christmas Past."

Scrooge rubbed his eyes, but the Ghost was still there. Although he was frightened, Scrooge did as the Ghost asked and got out of bed.

Suddenly, Scrooge found himself walking with the Ghost up a lonely road. Before them was a large and ancient building. Scrooge and the Ghost went through the door.

Inside, alone in a room, sat a young schoolboy. All the other boys had gone home for Christmas, and this child was left with only the schoolmaster for company. He seemed very sad indeed.

Scrooge saw the boy and said, "Why, that looks like me when I was young! I know just how it feels to be left alone at Christmas."

"Exactly," remarked the Ghost. "I am showing you your own Christmas of long ago. That's why I am called the Ghost of Christmas Past."

The next thing Scrooge knew, he was back in his bed. Then he heard another strange sound, and a second ghost appeared. "I am the Ghost of Christmas Present," said the figure.

Scrooge suddenly found himself looking into the home of his clerk, Bob Cratchit. The Cratchits were just finishing eating the smallest pudding Scrooge had ever seen, yet they laughed and smiled as if it were a feast fit for a king. They were celebrating Christmas, even though they had tea instead of wassail to drink and could not afford a Christmas turkey.

Bob Cratchit's youngest son, Tiny Tim, was so frail that he had to use a crutch. But he said to his brothers and sisters with a smile, "Merry Christmas to you, every one!"

*B*ack in his own bed again, Scrooge was soon visited by a third ghost, who said, "I am the Ghost of Christmas Yet-to-Come."

Just then, Scrooge saw three men strolling along a street on Christmas morning, talking to each other. "Yes, I hear that Scrooge is sick," said the first.

"Who cares what happens to him?" remarked the second.

The third man nodded in agreement. "Anyone who calls Christmas 'humbug' doesn't deserve our help," he said.

Scrooge realized they were talking about *him!*

The next thing he knew, Scrooge was back in bed and the morning sun was coming through the window. It was Christmas day.

As soon as he could get dressed, Scrooge hurried to the market and bought the biggest Christmas turkey he could find. Then he bought pies and cakes and puddings and fruit. He had them all sent to the Cratchits'.

Scrooge went back into the street. As he walked, he gave money to people along the way who seemed too poor to buy Christmas gifts for themselves or their families.

He passed the carolers that had visited his office the day before. They looked at him, first with surprise and then with smiles, as he called out a hearty "Merry Christmas!"

That Christmas Day, Scrooge went to shop after shop and bought Christmas gifts for every member of Bob Cratchit's family.

He bought dolls for the girls and balls for the boys. He bought warm scarves and mittens for all the children. For Mrs. Cratchit, he purchased a lovely handkerchief, and for Bob Cratchit a pair of handsome gloves. Best of all, for Tiny Tim he bought a toy puppet!

After he had gathered up all his gifts, he went to the Cratchits'. He burst in the door with his arms full of presents, crying, "Merry Christmas! Merry Christmas!"

Scrooge and the Cratchit family had a Christmas dinner none would ever forget. That night, they ate their fill of turkey with all the trimmings, then opened their gifts.

As they all sat round the fire, Tiny Tim looked at the happy, smiling faces and said, "Merry Christmas! God bless us, every one!"

THE
Wishing Star

*D*avey looked out the window at the falling snow. Usually he loved snow, but today he was sad. It was Christmas Eve, and the snow was so deep that it might ruin Christmas for Davey.

Because of the snowstorm, Davey was afraid that his older brother Josh would never make it home for Christmas.

"And I have such a special present for him!" Davey said to himself. "If only he could get here!"

With his best crayons, Davey had drawn a picture of the barn on their farm. He was going to give it to Josh for Christmas to hang in his room at college. Davey turned away from the window with a sigh.

*J*ust then, Dad called, "How about some help shoveling the driveway? We're going to try to make it into town to finish our Christmas shopping. We also have to buy our tree, don't forget."

Davey ran to get his boots and coat. He followed Dad out into the snow. Davey picked up his small shovel and set to work, while Dad used his bigger one. Helping Dad shovel the snow made Davey feel better.

Soon, Davey and Dad and Mom were on their way to town. Because of the snow, they had to drive slowly.

"I brought my picture for Josh with me," Davey said as they rode along. "Maybe I can find a frame to fit it when we get to the store."

"Good idea," said Mom. "I'll help you look."

When they got to town, they went to the Christmas tree lot. Davey was the first one out of the car. He ran over to a beautiful, glossy, tall tree.

"Look at this one!" he shouted to Mom and Dad. "Josh will love this tree!" Then he remembered. Josh probably wouldn't be home at all. Davey felt sad again.

Mom and Dad came over to see the tree Davey had found. "That's a great tree, Davey," said Dad with a smile. "I think you're right. It's the one we should get."

Mom added, "And even if Josh doesn't get here to see it, he'd still be happy we have such a beautiful tree."

*L*ater, at the store, Mom took Davey to the counter where picture frames were sold. Davey looked at all the frames. Finally he said, "I like this wooden one. It reminds me of the wooden barn in my picture."

The wooden frame was just the right size for his picture. Davey was very pleased. "I'm getting this just in case Josh makes it home for Christmas," he said.

Mom patted him on the shoulder. "I know how much you want Josh to be here tonight," she said, "but it is still snowing hard. I really don't think he'll make it. So you mustn't be too disappointed."

"At least I can wish he'd come," Davey said.

As they were about to leave the store, Davey saw a crowd of people. "What are all those people looking at?" Davey wondered. He ran to get a closer look. Looking around the man in front of him, Davey could see what was at the center of the crowd.

It was Santa! Children were sitting on Santa's lap and talking to him. "Can we get in line, please Dad?" begged Davey.

"Well, we're kind of in a hurry. We need to be back home before the snow gets too deep," said Dad. "But since this is Santa, I guess we can spare the time."

Davey gave Dad a big thank-you hug and ran to get in line. It seemed to take forever, but at last it was his turn.

When Davey climbed up on Santa's lap, Santa said, "Well, well, and what would you like for Christmas?"

"I wish my brother Josh could get home for Christmas," Davey said. "But the snow is so deep that Mom and Dad don't think he can make it."

"I don't usually deliver people on Christmas Eve, just toys," said Santa. "But I'll tell you what. Tonight, before you go to sleep, make your wish on the biggest, brightest star in the sky. That's the Wishing Star."

"Will it really work?" Davey asked Santa.

"Well, you never can tell about wishes, so I don't make any guarantees," said Santa. "But it surely doesn't hurt to try!"

On the way home in the car, Davey saw that the snow was coming down harder and harder. When he and Mom and Dad were almost to the house, Davey talked about Santa's Wishing Star.

"We all make wishes every now and then," said Mom, "but sometimes they just can't come true."

"I'm going to try, anyway," insisted Davey.

That night after dinner, Dad put the Christmas tree in its stand, and Mom and Davey joined him in decorating it with colored lights and balls and lots of tinsel.

While they were working, Davey thought sadly, "It would be so great if Josh were here to see our beautiful tree."

*D*ad put the golden angel on the very top. "I think this is the best tree we've ever had!" he exclaimed.

Davey went over to the window and looked out. The snow had stopped falling. And there, right overhead, was a star Davey had never seen before. It was big and bright and sparkling. It was the biggest and brightest star in the sky, just as Santa had said.

Davey looked at the star and said, "Wishing Star, please let my Christmas wish come true. I wish that Josh would come home tonight, so we can all be together for Christmas." Then Davey closed his eyes and wished as hard as he could.

*T*oo soon, Davey heard Mom's voice. "Time for bed, little one. If you go right to sleep, it will be Christmas morning before you know it."

Davey hung his stocking by the fireplace. He kissed Mom and Dad and started up the stairs to his room.

Just then, the three of them heard a sound outside the front door. "Who could that be?" asked Dad.

Suddenly, the door flew open, and there was Josh! Davey raced to the door, flung his arms around his brother, and gave him the biggest hug he could manage.

Josh had made it home after all. Davey's Christmas wish had come true!

*L*ater that night, when Davey was finally in bed, he looked out his window. Sure enough, the Wishing Star was still high in the sky.

"Thank you, Wishing Star," he whispered. "I knew you could do it. You've made this my best Christmas ever!"

THE LITTLE
Match Girl

*T*he weather was frosty and cold. It was growing dark, and a heavy snow had begun to fall. It was Christmas Eve.

A little girl wandered in the darkening steets. She wore ragged clothes, and she carried a bundle of matches in her hand.

All day, the Little Match Girl had been trying to sell her matches. "A penny for a match!" she had called in a small, pitiful voice to shoppers on the streets.

But the people just glanced at her and then hurried on their way. Now it was almost night. The poor girl had not sold a single match.

As she walked along, the Little Match Girl grew very cold. She wore only an old, thin pair of slippers. She had no socks, for she could not afford them.

Suddenly, a voice bellowed, "Out of my way!" At that moment, she heard the thundering sound of horses' hooves. She scurried across the street, barely managing to get out of the way of a large carriage pulled by two enormous horses.

When she stopped to catch her breath, the Little Match Girl looked down at her feet. In fleeing the carriage and horses, she had lost her slippers. Now the Little Match Girl had no shoes at all.

*T*he Little Match Girl wandered through the streets as the hour grew later and later. Up ahead, she saw a light shining through the window of one of the houses.

The Little Match Girl looked in the window and saw a table spread with a white tablecloth and set with candles and silver. On the table was a grand Christmas feast—a fat goose stuffed with the traditional apples and nuts, cakes and pies of all sorts, puddings, and every imaginable fruit. The Little Match Girl had never beheld such a feast.

A family came into the room and sat down at the table. The little girl wished that she could join the mother, father, and three young ones who were about to eat this beautiful Christmas dinner. How hungry she was!

*T*he Little Match Girl sighed and turned away, then continued down the street. Soon she saw a light shining from the window of another house.

This time when she looked inside, the Little Match Girl saw an extraordinarily lovely Christmas tree. There was a gold star at the top, and candles flickered on the branches. Gaily wrapped packages were piled beneath the tree.

While the Little Match Girl watched, a group of joyous girls and boys entered the room. They clapped their hands with delight when they saw the tree and all the presents.

How the Little Match Girl wished she could have laughed and played with the children around the Christmas tree!

As she turned away from the window, the Little Match Girl heard singing from a group of carolers nearby:

Silent night, holy night,
All is calm, all is bright. . . .

The Little Match Girl thought the music so beautiful that she followed the carolers down the street listening to their song:

'Round yon Virgin Mother and Child,
Holy Infant so tender and mild.
Sleep in heavenly peace,
Sleep in heavenly peace.

When they finished singing, the carolers were invited to come inside a brightly lit kitchen. Standing near the door, the Little Match Girl could smell bread baking inside. Once again, she was all alone.

Now it was growing late, and the Little Match Girl was very cold. To keep warm, she decided to light one of her matches.

She struck the match, and the light flared. In the bright glow of the match, she imagined herself sitting at a table eating a Christmas feast just like the one she had seen through the lighted window.

The Little Match Girl was eating Christmas goose, with pudding and fruit and cake and pie. How warm and full and happy she was!

Just then, the match went out. The bright light was gone, and the Little Match Girl was alone again in the dark. She shivered with cold.

The Little Match Girl decided to light a second match to try to get warm again. She struck the match, and once more a warm glow and bright light appeared.

In the light from this match, she saw herself with the boys and girls around the Christmas tree. She was about to open a Christmas gift wrapped in red paper and tied with a gold ribbon. She was anxious to see what might be inside.

Just then, the match burned out. Suddenly, everything was dark, and again the Little Match Girl was cold and alone.

*E*xcept for the light from streetlamps, the night was utterly dark, and the Little Match Girl grew so cold that she decided to light the entire bundle of matches.

When she struck all her matches, the whole world suddenly seemed to light up. Stars shot down from the sky. The Little Match Girl felt warm and wonderful.

As she looked around, the Little Match Girl had an amazing vision. She saw an angel dressed all in white. The angel was smiling and coming toward her with outstretched arms.

he angel picked the Little Match Girl up in her arms and smiled upon the small face. The angel started to walk, carrying the Little Match Girl.

"Where are we going?" asked the girl.

"I am taking you to a place where you will never be cold," the angel replied as they rose slowly into the night sky. "It is a place always filled with light and warmth. We will go where there are only laughter and smiles, and where you will never be hungry again."

*T*he next morning, those who emerged from their houses saw the bundle of burnt matches lying in the snow. They wondered what had happened.

What they could not know was that the Little Match Girl had gone to a place where she would always be warm and loved and happy—*so* happy that every single day would seem just like Christmas!

THE
Christmas
Mouse

*W*alter Whiskers was a sad little mouse. This big house was his home. In fact, he had lived in a mouse hole in this very same house since he was a tiny mousekin himself.

His little mouse hole had always been a warm, cozy place. And there was always plenty to eat— at least, up until a few months ago. Then, the family that lived here had moved out.

Now there were no children in the house, no music or parties or fun anymore. And there were no good things to eat. Walter sighed, thinking how much he missed it all.

*W*alter lived in the house with his wife, Wanda Whiskers, and their four mousekin children, Willie, Warner, Wilma, and little Winifred.

They used to be well-fed and happy, because there were always scraps of food to pick up off the kitchen floor or from under the dining room table. And there were usually delicious tidbits to be found behind the kitchen stove.

But now, Walter and his family grew each day more hungry and cold. And to top it all off, Christmas was coming! What was Walter to do?

*T*hen, just two days before Christmas, something happened. Wanda shook Walter awake early. "What is that noise!" she exclaimed. They heard banging and shouting right outside their mouse hole door. Walter ran to the door and looked out.

There were people moving into their house! Rugs and chairs and a large green sofa were being carried into the big living room. And a huge piano was taking up one whole corner.

As Walter watched, three children ran in. They were laughing and looking around excitedly. One of them said, "Oh, I'm going to love our new house!"

*W*alter called for his whole family to come and see the sight. Wanda and all the little mousekins were delighted to have a new family moving into their house.

"Now there will be plenty of food for us, and our mouse hole will be warm again," Walter told Wanda and the children. "It will be just like in the old days, you'll see."

But Walter didn't know what a terrible commotion and racket all that furniture moving would make! The whole mouse hole shook with the noise. The floor seemed to dance. And that night, there was still no food for the little mice.

But the next morning, the Whiskers family woke up to heavenly smells. And there was nice, warm air coming into the mouse hole. Today was Christmas Eve, and the new family was getting ready for its celebration.

That afternoon, Walter sniffed a different smell. He peeked out of the mouse hole, and again he called Wanda and the little mousekins to come and look.

The family was putting up a huge, beautiful Christmas tree! It reached all the way to the tall ceiling. And they were decorating it with sparkling lights and balls of all colors. At the top of the tree was a gold star.

That night, after the children had hung up their stockings and gone to bed, Walter and his family crept out into the living room to have a look around. They saw the most amazing sight!

"Look, Papa," cried little Winifred. There, running all the way around the Christmas tree, was a tiny toy train—just their size. It had a big red-and-orange engine, with three cars—blue, green, and orange—behind it, plus a red caboose at the end. The tracks for the train went over a bridge and around a toy mountain.

Beside the train was a tiny toy village. There were trees and shops and even a mouse-size house. Walter and his family could scarcely believe their eyes.

*W*alter said, "I know what we must do. Let's have a Christmas party of our own!"

"Oh, yes!" cried all the little mousekins. At that, Wanda ran back into the mouse hole to get some old beads she had been saving. The mice hung the beads on a tiny tree to decorate it. They were of beautiful colors and looked like shiny balls on the little tree.

Then Willie remembered some apple seeds he had. The mousekins strung them together to make more decorations for the tree. Wanda even cut a scrap of gold paper in the shape of a tiny star to put on top. Now they had their very own Christmas tree!

*T*hen Walter went into the dining room where the family had eaten its Christmas Eve dinner. He gathered crumbs from beneath the table. There were bits of delicious cheese, scraps of tasty bread, and even tiny morsels of cake. What a feast the Whiskers family had!

Finally, Walter said, "We must have one last treat to celebrate our good fortune. We will all take a ride on the train. And I will be the engineer."

So Walter climbed up into the train's engine, while Wanda and the little mousekins piled into the cars behind. Willie insisted on sitting in the caboose. And they rode all the way 'round and 'round the Christmas tree!

*F*inally, Walter said, "It is time for all you little mousekins to be in bed. We have had the best Christmas celebration ever!"

"Oh, yes, Papa!" cried Willie and Warner and Wilma and Winifred.

Next morning, the children of the house ran downstairs to see their stockings. They looked at the train and toy village. The tiny tree had Christmas decorations on it. And there were small crumbs scattered around. Little paw prints led to the train.

Their father smiled and said, "It looks as if someone else enjoyed our Christmas, too. Why, I believe we have our very own Christmas mouse!"

*D*eep inside his mouse hole, Walter Whiskers smiled. He was thinking of last night's Christmas treat and of the many wonderful Christmases to come.

Jingle Bells

*T*oby was mad. "It isn't fair!" he said as he stomped around the kitchen. "Why does it always happen this way?" he asked his mother.

Jeb and Harriet, his big brother and sister, always had all the fun. And tonight they were going out again on a sleigh ride with the older boys and girls from some of the farms nearby.

Toby couldn't go along because he was "too little." Would he ever not be "too little" for all the things he wanted to do? "When will I be big enough, Mama? That's what I want to know."

Mama smiled. "Maybe next year you'll be big enough to go. But right now, it's time for bed," she said.

Toby went up to the bedroom he shared with baby Sarah. "Look how much bigger I am than Sarah. Why do Harriet and Jeb always do things together, and I get stuck with the baby?" he complained.

But Mama just hugged Toby and smiled again. "Some day you'll be big. I promise you that," she said. Then she tucked Toby and Sarah under their warm quilts and kissed them goodnight.

*J*ust as Toby closed his eyes, he heard a jingling noise outside. He jumped out of bed and looked out the window of his room just in time to see Harriet and Jeb climbing into a sleigh. It was pulled by a beautiful chestnut horse.

The sleigh was full of laughing boys and girls dressed in hats and mittens and heavy scarves. The horse stamped its hooves, and the boy driving the sleigh called, "Come on, Harriet and Jeb. What a ride we're going to have tonight!"

As the sleigh pulled away from the door of the house, Toby could hear the riders sing, "Dashing through the snow, In a one-horse open sleigh. . . ."

*T*he next day was Christmas Eve. Papa called to Harriet and Jeb, "We have an important job to do this morning. We must go to the woods and cut down our Christmas tree."

"I'll come, too!" shouted Toby.

"You'd better stay here with Mama and Sarah," said Papa. "Maybe next year you'll be big enough to help." Toby was so disappointed that tears came to his eyes. Then Mama had an idea! While the others went for the tree, she and Toby made long strings of red cranberries for decorations. Little Sarah watched them. She kept laughing and trying to grab the cranberries. It wasn't such a bad morning after all.

*J*ust before lunch, Papa and Harriet and Jeb
came stomping into the house, half covered
with snow. They were dragging a huge tree.
"Let's hurry and eat our lunch," said Papa, "so we
can get this tree decorated."

That afternoon, Papa set up the tree in the
parlor. The whole family gathered to put colored
balls and sparkling tinsel on it.

Then Toby said, "Look what Mama and I made
this morning for our tree." He proudly brought in
his strings of cranberries. Jeb helped him hang
them from even the tallest branches. Toby was
sure that his decorations were the prettiest ones
of all.

*T*hat night, Harriet and Jeb and Toby all hung their stockings on the fireplace. Harriet hung up one of her long, blue stockings. Jeb's brown stocking had a hole in the toe. He hoped none of his presents would fall through the hole! Toby hung up his favorite green stocking. They also put up a little red-and-white-striped one for baby Sarah because she was too small to do it herself.

Then Mama said, "Now it's off to bed for Toby and Sarah."

"This early?" said Toby. He thought about begging to stay up just a little longer. But for once, he didn't protest. Because, after all, tomorrow would be Christmas!

ut after Toby was in bed, he had barely closed his eyes when Papa and Mama came into the bedroom. Could it be time to get up already?

"Don't go to sleep quite yet, little ones," Papa said to Toby and Sarah. "Mama and Harriet and Jeb and I have a big surprise for you."

Mama and Papa carried Sarah and Toby, both of them wrapped in the warm quilts, to the door of their house. There, right in front of the house, was a beautiful sleigh! It was painted red and was decorated with little round silver bells. Quickly, the whole family piled into the sleigh. Bells tinkled as they slowly started to glide across the snow.

Soon they were speeding along in the open fields to the clip-clop of horse's hooves and the jingling of bells. It seemed to Toby that they must be flying! And as they rode, they began to sing:

Dashing through the snow,
In a one-horse open sleigh,
O'er the fields we go,
Laughing all the way.
Bells on bobtail ring,
Making spirits bright,
What fun it is to ride and sing
A sleighing song tonight!

Jingle bells! Jingle bells!
Jingle all the way!
Oh, what fun it is to ride
In a one-horse open sleigh!

As they started back toward home, Papa slowed the horse to an easy trot. The swaying of the sleigh and the tinkling of the bells made it hard for Toby to keep his eyes open.

Toby leaned his head against Papa's big shoulder. He smiled up at Papa and whispered, "This is the best Christmas surprise I've ever had!"

*A*nd as Toby's eyes slowly shut in sleep, he hummed to himself, "Jingle all the way. . . ."

THE MAGIC
Toy Shop

Snow covered the ground, and more snowflakes were falling softly. It was growing dark. Only a streetlamp lit the front of the toy shop. Inside, the old toymaker Cornelius was busy working.

"Only two more days left 'til Christmas," Cornelius muttered to himself. "I still have all these toys to finish before the big day. I'm not as young as I used to be, and I can't work as fast. I just hope I'll be able to finish them."

Cornelius knew that the boys and girls in his town were looking forward to receiving their Christmas toys. And he had made a special one for each child he knew.

*J*ust then, Cornelius's wife Katerina entered the shop. "It is past time for you to come home for your supper," she said kindly. "You must quit for tonight."

"I can't stop now. I must keep working," said Cornelius. "I have to finish this toy train before I can stop for supper. Little Charles will be disappointed if he doesn't have his train for Christmas."

Cornelius pointed to a doll and a pair of skates he had just finished. "At least those are ready for Caroline and little Tommy," he said. "But I still have to make the wooden toy soldier for Edward. Christmas seems to get busier every year."

At that moment, the bell on the shop door tinkled. A poor woman came in with her three children. The children's eyes opened wide as they gazed at the wonderful toys.

"Look at that toy train!" said the oldest boy, Peter. "How I wish I could have it for my very own." Lisa, his sister, smiled shyly at the beautiful princess doll. Little Karen touched the cuddly pink bunny.

But the mother sighed. She had only a few pennies to spend, certainly not enough for these wonderful toys. Sadly, she and the children left the shop.

After the children and their mother left, Katerina was unhappy. Then she had an idea. "Why don't we give the children the toys they want," she said, "as a special Christmas gift, even if they can't pay for them?"

Old Cornelius shook his head sadly. "I wish we could. But those toys are already promised to other children. And I have no time left to make any more."

So Cornelius carefully put all his tools away. Then he and Katerina closed the shop and went out into the snowy night.

After Cornelius and Katerina left, the toys in the little shop suddenly seemed to awaken and come to life. They began talking among themselves. They had heard and seen the poor children wishing for Christmas toys.

Then Harold, one of the most handsome of the toy soldiers, had an idea. "We can help. We can make the special gifts for the children for Christmas!"

"Oh, yes!" cried Brown Bear. "I'll make the softest, most cuddly pink rabbit ever for little Karen."

"And we'll get started right now on the toy train for Peter," said Hans and William, two strong and clever toy soldiers.

But Louisa, the beautiful doll, said, "What foolish ideas you have! I have never done any work before, and I'm sure I won't begin now. You silly toys go right ahead, if you think you can. But don't count on me!"

She walked over to the corner of the toy shelf and watched as the other toys began to work.

Hans and William, the two toy soldiers, were already busy putting together the engine of a toy train. Harold came over to help them. Brown Bear was sewing up the sides of a pink, furry bunny. He called to Veronica, a gray elephant with lavender ears, to bring over plenty of soft stuffing.

*T*hen Louisa looked up to see two taffy-colored kittens trying to paint a face on a princess doll. They were dripping paint everywhere.

"Goodness," thought Louisa, "can't they do any better than that? They're making a terrible mess of it. Maybe I had better help them, just for a little while."

Louisa shooed the kittens away and set to work herself. After a while, one of the kittens said, "Oooh, how beautiful you've made her—almost as beautiful as you are!" Louisa just smiled her beautiful smile and patted the kittens on the head.

*W*hen Cornelius and Katerina opened their shop the next day, they saw three toys they had never seen before. There was a train, with a tag that said *To Peter*. And a princess doll, with a tag reading *To Lisa*. And, finally, a pink stuffed bunny, whose tag said *To Little Karen*.

"Where did these come from?" Cornelius wondered aloud. "I can't understand it. Something magical must have happened here!"

That evening, when the mother and her three children passed the shop again, Cornelius called to them to come inside. Then he and Katerina gave them their wonderful Christmas gifts.

*C*ornelius and Katerina did not come to their shop the next day because it was Christmas. They stayed home to eat their own special Christmas dinner. They were happy because they knew that all the children in town were playing with their new Christmas toys.

But the very next day, when Cornelius came to his toy shop, he took down the sign over the door. "What are you doing?" asked Katerina.

"I must change the name of my shop," he said. "I will make a new sign. From now on, my shop will not be called *The Toy Shop*."

W hat will you call it, then?" asked Katerina.

"Because of the magical thing that happened this Christmas," said Cornelius, "from now on my shop will be called *The Magic Toy Shop!*"

THE
Littlest
Angel

A very long time ago, long before anybody on earth today was born, there was no Christmas season—no gaily decorated Christmas trees, no yuletide gift-giving, no carolers singing on a snowy December night. That's because it was a time before the birth of Jesus in a lowly stable in Bethlehem.

There was such a thing as Heaven, of course, the home of glorious angels who sailed the skies on beautiful white-feathered wings. They wore long, flowing white gowns, and their golden hair fell in waves and curls down their backs.

They were tall and strong and swift—all except the Littlest Angel, who was tiny, with short, curly blonde locks. She had just got her wings and was only now learning to fly.

One day, Archangel Gabriel made an important announcement. "Tonight," declared Gabriel in a ringing voice, "we fly to earth to honor the birth of the Prince of Peace! We will sing hymns throughout the world, giving tidings of great joy!"

The Littlest Angel jumped up and down with excitement. Tonight was the night she had heard so much about! For weeks, the big angels had been planning a splendid celebration.

Would she be allowed to go along? The Littlest Angel's singing voice was still weak, but she had a worse problem: She couldn't fly as fast as the others. It did not look promising.

"*Unless* I get a head start," she thought, and this cheered her up. "If I go now, I'll be in Bethlehem before the others get there. Won't they be surprised to see me!"

At that moment, the Littlest Angel happened to be strolling beside Heaven's crystal sea. On the shore grew thousands of starflowers with their golden centers and five pearl-white petals.

Starflowers were valued on earth as a sign of hope and would surely make a lovely gift for the newborn infant. So the Littlest Angel gathered a bunch and stuck them inside the sash of her robe.

It was time to test her wings in a way they'd never been tested before. The Littlest Angel climbed atop the highest cloud, then jumped!

Miraculously, her baby wings spread wide, and the Littlest Angel glided in the bright air. Now the wings began to beat, and she aimed for planet Earth down below.

When the Littlest Angel landed, she looked around. Where did Bethlehem lie? The sun was setting, and there was no one in sight. But then in the distance she saw a village with houses of mud brick and stone, so she headed down the dirt road toward it.

On the way, the Littlest Angel heard a pitiful sound from a nearby olive tree. A mother dove was cooing sadly from a high branch. Below, her baby, which had fallen from its nest, was struggling to fly but with no success. It was too young. The Littlest Angel picked up the birdling.

"You poor thing," she said. Up the Littlest Angel flew and settled the little dove gently in the nest. The mother thanked her with all her heart. A starflower fell from the Littlest Angel's sash and landed where the dove had fallen. Suddenly, a bell rang out through the winter evening.

*T*he Littlest Angel came to a one-room hut and peered inside a window. There sat a careworn young mother watching over her little son, who slept fitfully in a cradle.

The Littlest Angel could see the child's skin was hot and damp, and tendrils of hair clung to his cheeks and forehead. The mother rocked the cradle and wept softly to herself.

The child opened his feverish eyes and smiled as the Littlest Angel tiptoed in. The angel laid a cool hand on the boy's forehead, and the fever went away instantly. Soon the child closed its eyes and slept soundly.

As the Littlest Angel walked back through the door, a few starflowers fell from her sash, and a second bell rang out. It had grown dark, so she left the village and continued down the road.

The Littlest Angel's wings ached too much to fly. She had no idea where she was headed, and she was so tired that she almost forgot why she had visited earth in the first place.

She was lost, too. Where was Bethlehem? The Littlest Angel seemed no nearer to the end of her journey than when she began, and she now had only a single starflower left. This troubled her. "What will happen if I lose this, too?" she thought. "I'll have nothing to give Jesus."

As if to make matters worse, the Littlest Angel stubbed her toe on a stone in the road. She hopped around, holding her injured foot. Suddenly overhead, a host of angels flew past, singing "Glory to God in the highest, and on earth peace to men of good will!"

"Oh, no!" cried the Littlest Angel. "I'm too late!"

A short time later, the Littlest Angel heard the sound of bleating nearby. In the bushes beside the road lay a little lamb that had broken its foreleg. She took pity on the suffering creature and gathered it up in her arms.

"Come with me to Bethlehem," said the angel, "that is, if I can ever find it!" The last starflower slipped unnoticed from her sash and fell in the dirt road. A third bell rang out through the night.

The Littlest Angel carried her pitiful burden down the road, and it seemed to get heavier and heavier. Her arms and legs were sore with fatigue. At the moment that she thought she might have to stop and rest, the Littlest Angel glimpsed light shining from far off. The closer it got, the more it seemed to be coming from a stable.

"We'll stop there," whispered the Littlest Angel, for the lamb had fallen asleep in her arms.

When the angel and her little lamb got within a short distance of the stable, they were greeted by the most amazing sights and sounds.

On the ground, several people had gathered. They were mostly poor and humble, but three men bearing costly gifts rode camels and were dressed in rich robes. The people were oddly quiet, but every now and then the Littlest Angel heard hushed words being spoken in strange languages.

Overhead in the velvet darkness flew scores of angels in a fiery blaze of light. Some were singing hymns, while others played shiny brass horns.

High above shone a single star, brighter and steadier than any the Littlest Angel had ever seen.

The Littlest Angel walked through the stable's bright doorway and was so astonished by what she saw that she nearly dropped the lamb.

There, in the straw, sat a pale but beautiful young woman holding a newborn infant in her arms. A bearded man wearing robes dusty from travel looked on. The Littlest Angel knew at once that she was in the presence of Jesus and his parents, Mary and Joseph. She laid the lamb in the straw and reached for her last starflower, but it wasn't there!

Mary smiled lovingly on the Littlest Angel. "I know what you're thinking," she said sweetly, "but you have brought a far greater gift—a creature in need." The baby Jesus reached out and, with his dimpled hand, touched the lamb's broken leg. Instantly the animal leaped up and frisked about.

"Not only that," added Mary, "but your good deeds have caused the Chime of Love to ring out three times tonight. Because of this, I ask that you visit every year and bring this music to people of good will."

The Littlest Angel was overjoyed. Such an important responsibility for one so little! She flew back to Heaven in a burst of speed.

And every Christmas, you'll hear this magical bell ring out—that is, if you've been kind and good throughout the year!

THE TWELVE DAYS OF
Christmas

On the first day of Christmas
my true love gave to me
A partridge in a pear tree.

On the second day of Christmas
  my true love gave to me
Two turtle doves
And a partridge in a pear tree.

On the third day of Christmas
  my true love gave to me
Three French hens
Two turtle doves
And a partridge in a pear tree.

On the fourth day of Christmas
 my true love gave to me
Four calling birds
Three French hens
Two turtle doves
And a partridge in a pear tree.

On the fifth day of Christmas
  my true love gave to me
Five golden rings
Four calling birds
Three French hens
Two turtle doves
And a partridge in a pear tree.

On the sixth day of Christmas
   my true love gave to me
Six geese a-laying
Five golden rings
Four calling birds
Three French hens
Two turtle doves
And a partridge in a pear tree.

On the seventh day of Christmas
  my true love gave to me
Seven swans a-swimming
Six geese a-laying
Five golden rings
Four calling birds
Three French hens
Two turtle doves
And a partridge in a pear tree.

On the eighth day of Christmas
  my true love gave to me
Eight maids a-milking
Seven swans a-swimming
Six geese a-laying
Five golden rings
Four calling birds
Three French hens
Two turtle doves
And a partridge in a pear tree.

On the ninth day of Christmas
  my true love gave to me
Nine ladies dancing
Eight maids a-milking
Seven swans a-swimming
Six geese a-laying
Five golden rings
Four calling birds
Three French hens
Two turtle doves
And a partridge in a pear tree.

On the tenth day of Christmas
  my true love gave to me
Ten lords a-leaping
Nine ladies dancing
Eight maids a-milking
Seven swans a-swimming
Six geese a-laying
Five golden rings
Four calling birds
Three French hens
Two turtle doves
And a partridge in a pear tree.

On the eleventh day of Christmas
  my true love gave to me
Eleven pipers piping
Ten lords a-leaping
Nine ladies dancing
Eight maids a-milking
Seven swans a-swimming
Six geese a-laying
Five golden rings
Four calling birds
Three French hens
Two turtle doves
And a partridge in a pear tree.

On the twelfth day of Christmas
  my true love gave to me
Twelve drummers drumming
Eleven pipers piping
Ten lords a-leaping
Nine ladies dancing
Eight maids a-milking
Seven swans a-swimming
Six geese a-laying
Five golden rings
Four calling birds
Three French hens
Two turtle doves

And a partridge in a pear tree.

THE
Christmas
Bear

Kate looked out the window at the snow. "Fuzzy," she said to her toy bear, "aren't you excited? Today is Christmas Eve!"

Kate gave Fuzzy a hug. "Just think—tonight is the night Santa Claus comes!"

Kate's mother walked into the room. "Kate, get your coat and boots. We need to go to town for a few last-minute gifts. We still don't have a present for Mr. Noonan." This was the old gentleman who lived across the street.

Kate ran to get her winter jacket. "Can Fuzzy come with us?" she asked.

"I don't see why not," Mommy replied.

"Mommy," said Kate, as she and her mother went out into the snow, "Fuzzy needs a sweater and hat to wear this winter, too."

Kate held Fuzzy tightly as she followed Mommy around the department store. After they had bought a warm scarf for Mr. Noonan, they walked past the toy department.

"Mommy, can we please stop and look at the toys?" Kate asked. "I want Fuzzy to see them."

Kate held Fuzzy up to look. Fuzzy thought he had never seen so many amazing toys in all his life.

There were beautiful dolls, tall toy soldiers, and brightly painted toy trains. There were skates and sleds, dollhouses and doll furniture, and more stuffed animals than Fuzzy could have imagined. He saw rabbits, elephants, giraffes, puppies, kittens—even some bears that looked a little like him!

Kate said, "All the toys in this store are wonderful, Fuzzy, but no one is as special as you. You've been with me ever since I can remember! Every night when I go to sleep, you're there. And every morning when I wake up, you're still there." She squeezed Fuzzy. "I love you!"

Fuzzy smiled to himself. He remembered the time Kate had had the measles. She was feverish at first, and then there were red spots all over her face. But he cuddled up with her anyway to make her feel better.

Fuzzy also thought about the birthday party Kate had given for him. All her other dolls had come, but the birthday cake was made special for him. "What a lucky bear I am," he said to himself.

Then Kate and Fuzzy got in line to talk to Santa Claus. The line moved slowly, as each child sat in Santa's lap to whisper in his ear. Finally, it was Kate's turn. She put Fuzzy on the floor and climbed onto Santa's lap.

Kate told Santa all about her family. She told him what a good time they had every year making Christmas cookies and decorating their tree. She told him to look for the plate of cookies and glass of milk that she planned to set out for him that night.

Santa asked, "What would you like for Christmas, Kate?"

Kate smiled and said, "I'd like to have a new red sweater and hat for my favorite friend, my bear Fuzzy."

When Kate finished talking to Santa, she ran back to her mother. "Mommy, Mommy, guess what I said to Santa!" She was so busy telling Mommy all about it that she didn't notice she had left Fuzzy lying on the floor.

Kate and her mother hurried home. It was getting late, and all the stores were closing. But just as they walked into the house, Kate cried, "Where's Fuzzy?"

"Don't you have him?" asked Mommy.

"Oh, no!" said Kate. "Did we leave him at the store?"

It was too late to go back and try to find poor Fuzzy. Kate was broken-hearted. "I can't lose Fuzzy!" She began to cry.

At the very moment Kate was sobbing for her lost bear, poor Fuzzy was feeling pretty sad himself as he sat on the floor of the department store. He was lost and alone. What on earth could he do? A tear rolled down his cheek.

Then he heard a voice behind him. "What's the matter, little bear?" Fuzzy looked around and saw a tall toy soldier made of wood.

Fuzzy told the soldier what had happened to him. The soldier said, "Let's go and ask the other toys what you should do."

When they got to the toy department, Fuzzy told the other toys how he had been lost. The purple polka-dot stuffed elephant had an idea. "I know," he cried. "You must go outside the store and wait for Santa to come by tonight in his sleigh. Santa will surely help you."

"What's all this about Santa Claus and Christmas?" Fuzzy asked. "I really don't understand." Fuzzy was a young bear, and he didn't know much about the world.

A pretty little girl doll spoke up. "Oh, Christmas is wonderful," she said. "On Christmas morning, children everywhere wake up and find toys under the Christmas tree."

"How do the toys get there?" asked Fuzzy.

"Silly bear," giggled a blue stuffed rabbit. "Don't you know that Santa brings them?"

"And Santa will come to town tonight?" asked Fuzzy.

"Yes," replied the stuffed elephant. "That's why you must wait outside. He'll find you there."

Now it was nighttime. Fuzzy opened the front door and went bravely out into the dark to wait for Santa and his sleigh.

Fuzzy sat down in the snow. It was very cold. He waited and waited. He was sure he would never see Santa.

But, just as he was about to lose hope, Fuzzy heard a faint jingle in the distance. He looked again and, sure enough, Santa's sleigh was speeding right toward him! Reindeer were pulling the sleigh, with red-nosed Rudolph in the lead.

When Santa saw Fuzzy, he scooped him up and cried, "Fuzzy! I'm so glad I've found you! I have a new red sweater and hat for you—just the kind Kate asked for!"

*T*he next morning, Kate woke up and reached over in bed to hug Fuzzy. But he wasn't there!

Then she remembered. Fuzzy was lost. And today was Christmas Day. Santa had probably left a beautiful red sweater and hat for Fuzzy. But now there was no little brown bear to wear them.

Just then, Mommy and Daddy came in. "Merry Christmas, darling!" said Mommy.

"Fuzzy isn't here," Kate said sadly.

"Sweetie, why don't you go downstairs and look under the tree?" said Daddy.

Kate put on her robe and slippers and hurried down the stairs. And there, beneath the Christmas tree, was Fuzzy, dressed in a bright red sweater and stocking cap! Kate picked him up and hugged him with all her might.

"Oh, Fuzzy, I'm so glad to see you!" Kate cried with happiness. "And look at your new sweater and hat!"

Fuzzy smiled to himself. It was wonderful to be home again! He was proud to have such jaunty new clothes to wear—and especially happy to be Kate's Christmas Bear!

"I'm never going to lose you again!" Kate promised, and that made Fuzzy smile even more.

It was the best Christmas ever!

'TWAS THE NIGHT BEFORE
Christmas

'Twas the night before Christmas,
    when all through the house
Not a creature was stirring,
    not even a mouse.
The stockings were hung
    by the chimney with care,
In hopes that Saint Nicholas
    soon would be there.
The children were nestled
    all snug in their beds,
While visions of sugarplums
    danced in their heads;

And mamma in her kerchief,
　　and I in my cap,
Had just settled our brains
　　for a long winter's nap—
When out on the lawn
　　there arose such a clatter
I sprang from my bed
　　to see what was the matter.
Away to the window
　　I flew like a flash,
Tore open the shutter,
　　and threw up the sash.

The moon on the breast
of the new-fallen snow
Gave a luster of midday
to objects below;
When what to my
wondering eyes should appear
But a miniature sleigh
and eight tiny reindeer,
With a little old driver,
so lively and quick,
I knew in a minute
it must be Saint Nick!

More rapid than eagles
his coursers they came,
And he whistled and shouted
 and called them by name,
"Now, Dasher! now, Dancer!
 now, Prancer and Vixen!
On, Comet! on, Cupid!
 on, Donner, and Blitzen!—
To the top of the porch,
 to the top of the wall,
Now, dash away, dash away,
 dash away all!"

As dry leaves that before
    the wild hurricane fly,
When they meet with an obstacle
    mount to the sky,
So, up to the housetop
    the coursers they flew,
With a sleigh full of toys—
    and Saint Nicholas, too.
And then, in a twinkling,
    I heard on the roof,
The prancing and pawing
    of each little hoof.

As I drew in my head
   and was turning around,
Down the chimney Saint Nicholas
   came with a bound:
He was dressed all in fur
   from his head to his foot,
And his clothes were all tarnished
   with ashes and soot:
A bundle of toys
   he had flung on his back,
And he looked like a peddler
   just opening his pack.

His eyes, how they twinkled!
   his dimples, how merry!
His cheeks were like roses,
   his nose like a cherry;
His droll little mouth
   was drawn up like a bow,
And the beard on his chin
   was as white as the snow.

The stump of a pipe
   he held tight in his teeth,
And the smoke, it encircled
   his head like a wreath.
He had a broad face
   and a little round belly
That shook, when he laughed,
   like a bowl full of jelly.
He was chubby and plump—
   a right jolly old elf:
And I laughed when I saw him,
   in spite of myself;

A wink of his eye,
    and a twist of his head,
Soon gave me to know
    I had nothing to dread.
He spoke not a word,
    but went straight to his work,
And filled all the stockings:
    then turned with a jerk,
And laying a finger
    aside of his nose,
And giving a nod,
    up the chimney he rose.

He sprang to his sleigh,
    to his team gave a whistle,
And away they all flew
    like the down of a thistle.
But I heard him exclaim,
    ere they drove out of sight,
"Happy Christmas to all,
    and to all a good-night."

THE
Nutcracker

*I*t was Christmas Eve—at last! Every Christmas Eve, after dinner, Maria and her brother Fritz opened their presents. Even though Maria and Fritz lived in long-ago Germany, they also celebrated by giving gifts on this special day.

This evening, the Christmas tree in the parlor seemed even bigger and more beautiful than ever. And Maria and Fritz had wonderful presents. They had dolls, little toy soldiers, and picture books.

But Maria's favorite gift was from her godfather, Dr. Drosselmeier. It was a wooden nutcracker carved to look like an old soldier. It did not look like any other nutcracker Maria had ever seen. What Maria did not know, though, was that the nutcracker was enchanted!

After Maria and Fritz finished opening their presents, another celebration began. They were going to have an exciting Christmas party for their young cousins and friends. Everyone played with the dolls and toy soldiers, and there were all kinds of Christmas candies and cookies to eat.

Then Dr. Drosselmeier said, "Wait right here, children. I have a special Christmas treat for your party." Before the children could guess what the treat might be, he appeared with two puppets and a small stage for a puppet show.

The two puppets danced and leaped high off the stage and did somersaults, while the children watched and laughed and clapped. Maria held her favorite gift, the nutcracker, through the whole puppet show.

After the show was over, Fritz began to dance around just as the puppets had done. He grabbed the nutcracker from Maria and leaped up, holding it high. But Fritz could not dance quite as well as the puppets. He stumbled, and the nutcracker went flying across the room, landing near the Christmas tree.

When Maria ran to pick up her favorite gift, she saw that his wooden jaw was broken. "Oh, no!" she cried. "Let me fix you, poor nutcracker." She carefully tied the nutcracker back together with her handkerchief and put him under the Christmas tree.

Then Mother called, "It's time for bed." All the guests had left, and it was time to put out the lights and go upstairs.

*T*he house was quiet, but Maria could not sleep. She was thinking about the nutcracker under the Christmas tree.

Maria tiptoed downstairs. When she opened the doors to the big parlor, she was surprised to see that the Christmas tree was lighted again. She picked up her nutcracker, but he looked larger than when she had left him under the tree. And his jaw was not broken anymore!

The nutcracker seemed to be growing. As he grew taller and taller, his carved wooden face slowly changed. Before Maria's very eyes, the nutcracker became a handsome young prince. The Prince bowed to Maria and thanked her. Her act of kindness had broken a magic spell that had been cast over him.

*J*ust then, Maria heard a scuffling and scratching sound, with pattering and squeaking noises. She looked up to see a roomful of huge gray mice. "What are mice doing here?" wondered Maria.

The mice were led by a Mouse King, who had seven heads and carried a sword. Just as the Prince leaped in front of Maria to protect her, they heard the sounds of a trumpet and a drum.

Out of Fritz's gift box, left under the Christmas tree, sprang a whole troop of toy soldiers that grew to life size as soon as they stepped out of their box. The soldiers, led by the Prince, began a great battle with the Mouse King and his army of gray mice.

*W*hat a battle it was! Back and forth the two armies fought. Maria began to be afraid that the mice would win. The Prince and the toy soldiers seemed to be getting tired.

But just then Maria saw her chance to help. She took off her slipper and threw it with all her might at the Mouse King. Down he went! The battle was over. As quickly as they had come, the army of gray mice scampered away.

The Prince was now completely free from the magic spell. He could go home to his own land. "Would you come with me?" he asked Maria. "Oh, yes!" answered Maria.

So the Prince led Maria to the Christmas tree, which seemed to have grown taller. He raised his arms, and suddenly the Prince and Maria were no longer in Maria's parlor. Instead, they found themselves in the Nutcracker Prince's own kingdom. And all around them were beautiful dancing snow fairies.

"Welcome to the Land of Sweets," said the Prince. Maria saw sights she had never dreamed of. Here, the houses were made of chocolate and peppermint sticks. There was a river of lemonade, and a lake of sugar and almond milk.

Maria and the Prince traveled down the lemonade river, passing by lollipop trees and candy flowers. They rode in a little boat shaped like a seashell.

*F*inally, they arrived at a sparkling castle made entirely of spun sugar. This was the palace of the Sugar Plum Fairy, who came forth to greet them.

The Prince said, "Maria, with her kindness, has rescued me from an enchanted spell. In the battle with the Mouse King, at just the right moment, she attacked with her slipper and saved me."

When the Sugar Plum Fairy heard this, she invited Maria and the Prince to sit on her royal throne. She threw a great party to celebrate. Everyone in the Land of Sweets came! As tinkling music filled the hall, the Sugar Plum Fairy did a graceful fairy dance. Next came a parade of dancers—Chinese dancers, whirling Arabian dancers, leaping and twirling Russian dancers.

*M*aria had never seen such sights! There were chocolate dancers and pennywhistle candy dancers and even dancing clowns. Just when Maria could not imagine anything more grand, she was surrounded by enchanted flowers.

Everywhere she looked were beautiful flowers— buttercups and daffodils, roses and tulips. They seemed almost to float as they waltzed 'round and 'round the great ballroom.

Everyone joined in the dancing. Maria was a little afraid to dance. Then the Nutcracker Prince approached and said, "All this dancing is for you. You must dance, too. Come with me." So Maria and the Prince whirled and whirled and whirled . . .

. . . until Maria was a little dizzy and could no longer tell exactly where she was. She rubbed her eyes and sat up. She was beneath her own Christmas tree! In her own house. And here beside her was her nutcracker.

Where was the Prince? the dancers? the Sugar Plum Fairy? Oh, could it all have been a dream?

Santa Claus

IS COMING TO TOWN

Santa Claus was sitting at his desk, looking over his lists of children. Most of them had been very good all year, but there were a few he was worried about—especially Sam and Mike. "Well," said Santa Claus to his best helper, the elf Cornelius, "what's the latest news about Sam and Mike?"

"Well," said Cornelius, "they try hard to be good. But they seem to have a hard time. They get into trouble pretty easily."

"There are only four more days until I have to make my big trip," said Santa Claus. "We must decide about them soon."

"I'll keep my eye on them," said Cornelius. "I'll let you know how things are going."

Sam and Mike, the brothers Santa Claus and Cornelius had been discussing, ran into their kitchen. "It's four more days until Christmas," said Mike.

"No, it's not!" said Sam. "It's only three days!"

"It's four!" shouted Mike.

"No, three!" cried Sam.

"Boys!" said their mother. "Must you argue over every single thing?"

"Well, I'm right. . . ," started Mike.

"For once," laughed Mother, "you're both right. There are four days left until Christmas, if you count today as one of them. If you don't count today, then there are three."

Sam and Mike went into the living room, where their older sister Katie was playing. "I still say there are four days until Christmas," said Mike. "Right, Katie?"

"No, there are three, aren't there?" asked Sam.

"You two are always arguing," replied Katie. "Don't you know what happens to children who argue all the time?"

"What?" asked Sam and Mike.

"Well, in three—or four—days, Santa Claus will be coming. And he knows all about you two."

"What do you mean?" said Sam.

"Santa knows whether you've been good or bad. So you'd better watch out, you two!"

"Gee!" said Mike. "Maybe we should be careful. Okay, no more arguments. Let's go sledding." Sam and Mike got their coats and boots.

"Last one outside is a—! Oops, I forgot," said Sam.

Walking down the street, they passed Mr. Paulson's yard. "That's the best hill for sledding," said Mike. "Let's sneak in and sled down!"

"Mr. Paulson said he doesn't want anyone to sled in his yard," replied Sam. "But maybe just this one time wouldn't hurt."

Just as they were pushing off, who should look out the window but Mr. Paulson.

"What did I tell you boys!" he shouted from his door, waving his fist.

Meanwhile, Santa Claus decided to see how things were going in his workshop. The elves were working furiously. "Cornelius," called out Santa, "what's the latest news on those two mischief makers, Sam and Mike?"

Cornelius shook his head and told Santa about the boys' argument. He also said they had gone sledding in Mr. Paulson's yard. "Those boys," said Santa Claus sadly. "They do have a hard time being good." He looked around the workshop and asked, "What do they want for Christmas?"

Cornelius and another elf held up two toys. "Mike wants a toy train like this one, and Sam would like some ice skates," said Cornelius.

"Well, I sure hope I'll be able to deliver them," said Santa.

*I*t was just about this time that Sam and Mike were continuing on their way toward the park. "Maybe we'll find something fun to do there without getting into trouble," said Mike.

At the park, they found a group of boys building snow forts. The boys had chosen teams and were going to see who could build the biggest and best snow fort. Then they'd have a snowball fight.

"Let us help," called Mike and Sam.

"Sure, join in," said Charlie, one of the bigger boys. Just then, Sam noticed a little boy sitting by a tree, away from the other boys. He looked as if he had been crying.

"What's wrong with Joey?" Mike asked Charlie.

"Oh, Joey wanted to be on one of our teams," said Charlie, "but he's too little." Sam and Mike thought about that and decided they didn't agree.

"Hey, Joey!" called Sam. "Mike and I need someone just your size to reach the tough spots."

The three of them got to work. Soon their fort was as tall as the other ones. And then, with Mike and Sam lifting Joey up high to pile the snow on top, their fort stood even taller!

"Joey," called Charlie, "would you help our team a second? We need to get up high, too." With a big smile, Joey ran over to help Charlie's team.

A few days later, at the North Pole, Santa Claus was getting ready for his trip. The time had finally arrived—it was Christmas Eve! Santa had already hitched up his reindeer. "Cornelius," called Santa, "what is the latest news on Sam and Mike? I'm ready to pack their skates and train."

"Great news, Santa," said Cornelius. Then he told Santa Claus how Sam and Mike had asked Joey to help them build their snow fort, when none of the other boys would let Joey play.

Santa smiled his biggest smile of the day. "I knew they were good boys!" he exclaimed. "Sam and Mike did the most important thing—they were kind to another person. That's what really counts."

As Santa Claus was starting on his trip, his sleigh loaded with toys, Sam and Mike were getting ready for bed. They had hung up their stockings by the chimney. Cookies and milk were set out in case Santa wanted a snack.

After they were all tucked into bed, Mike whispered, "Hey, Sam, look out!" Just then, he threw his pillow across the room. It landed on Sam's head.

With a whoop, Sam yelled, "I'll get *you*!" He started to throw his own pillow back at Mike. But then he thought, "*Someone* knows whether I'm being good or not."

At that same moment, Mike remembered that *someone* knew when he was sleeping and when he was awake.

ike just whispered, "Good night, Sam, and Merry Christmas!" A hush fell over the room as they closed their eyes.

Late that night, while Mike and Sam slept, a smiling Santa laid a little toy train and some shiny new ice skates under the tree. If they had been awake, they would have heard a happy Santa say, "Well done, Mike and Sam! You were good, for goodness sake!"

THE
Tiny Elf

*T*here were only a few days left before Christmas. All of Santa's elves were working hard. Cornelius, the elf in charge of Santa's Workshop, was giving orders to the workers.

Some elves were busy at benches where they made dolls of all kinds. They also sewed beautiful costumes for the dolls to wear.

Another group made only the fastest toy trains. Others were proud of their skates and sleds.

"We need some more gold paint for our train engines," called one elf.

"And we're running out of carpeting for these doll houses," said another.

Santa's Workshop was a busy, busy place.

One of Santa's elves, though—a tiny elf named Casey—was not assigned to any of the workbenches in Santa's Workshop.

For years, Casey had been trying to show that he, too, could make beautiful toys. But every time he tried, things just went wrong.

"Let me paint that doll's face," he would plead. But when he tried, he smeared paint all over himself. And all over anyone or anything near him, too.

"I can build that dollhouse," he would say. But when he hammered, none of the nails ever seemed to go in straight.

Everyone loved little Casey. But, as Cornelius said, "That tiny elf will never be a toymaker!"

*E*very year, after Santa delivered toys to all the children, he came back to his workshop to thank the elves. They gathered around to hear how Rudolph had lighted the way for Santa's sleigh.

Cornelius said, "Remember when Tracy got that special baby doll she wanted?"

"And remember how Lamar loved that toy train we made?" said Winkie, another elf.

"Lisa really learned how to ice skate with those figure skates we made for her," added the elf Joey.

"Because of you, lots of children are happy every year," a smiling Santa told them. The elves clapped their hands in delight. It was the proudest moment of Christmas for Cornelius and his workers.

On this day before Christmas Eve, as the elves worked faster and faster, the door to the workshop suddenly swung open. And who should come through the door but Santa himself!

"How are things going?" he asked Cornelius.

"We're doing our best, Santa," said Cornelius. "We'll work late tonight, if we have to. I promise that we won't leave a single toy unfinished."

Santa looked at the thick sheaf of papers in his hand. "Here are the latest letters children have sent to me," he told Cornelius. "Just be sure we don't forget anyone."

Santa read through the letters, showing each one to Cornelius. They both checked to be sure every toy would be ready for the next night, Christmas Eve.

After Santa left, Cornelius went around from workbench to workbench, giving last-minute orders for toys. Casey followed him through the workshop.

"We're going to need another one of those trains with the big engines," he told the elf in charge of making all the toy trains.

"Oh, please let me make that train!" pleaded Casey, tugging on Cornelius's sleeve.

But Cornelius just smiled and patted Casey on the head. "I'd like to let you try, Casey. But we don't have time. Maybe next year."

Casey sighed. Why wouldn't they ever let him do anything important? He went over and sat down in one of the toy wagons. "It isn't fair," he said to himself.

*A*ll the elves worked late into the night. Cornelius walked through the workshop. "Is that sled ready for Eddie?" he called.

"Almost finished," shouted an elf who was busy putting the final coat of red paint on a sled.

"What about the dollhouse for Cherise?"

"I'm nailing the roof on it right now," came the answer from another elf.

Cornelius walked by a group of workers making stuffed animals. "Remember that Tina wants her teddy bear to be nice and soft," he warned.

Casey helped the other elves by running to get some more blue and yellow paint and by picking up dropped nails. But how he wished he could make a toy all by himself!

*F*inally, when the clock struck midnight, the weary elves finished the last toy. "Tomorrow," said Cornelius, "we only have to help Santa load up his sleigh." Tomorrow would be Christmas Eve.

As the elves filed out of Santa's Workshop, Casey turned back to take a final look at all the wonderful toys the elves had made.

But what was that piece of paper lying beneath Cornelius's desk? Casey ran back into the workshop and picked it up from the floor. "Oh, no!" he cried when he read it. The elves had forgotten one last toy!

The piece of paper was a letter from little Mattie, who wanted to be a dancer when she grew up. She was asking Santa to bring her a special ballerina doll for Christmas.

What was Casey to do? By now, the other elves were in bed, and it was too late to call them back to work. But poor Mattie—she would be terribly disappointed on Christmas Day!

Casey sat down on one of the toy wagons to think. Suddenly he had an idea. He would make the ballerina doll himself!

With that, Casey went to gather all the materials he would need. While the other elves slept, Casey worked through the night. He sawed and sanded. He painted and sewed.

Just as the morning sun peeked in the windows of the workshop, Casey held up his finished doll. He had made a beautiful ballerina with dark hair, sparkling eyes, a pink dancing costume, and pink ballet slippers! Now it was ready to pack on Santa's sleigh.

As always, when Santa finished his long Christmas Eve sleigh ride, he returned to his workshop. He had delivered the toys to children all over the world. Now he wanted to thank the hard-working elves.

This time, though, Santa said, "I want to thank one little elf in particular. Because of him, not a single child will be disappointed on Christmas morning. This elf stayed up all night to be sure no toy was forgotten.

"For his help," Santa said, "I have a special award for a special elf—Casey!" At that, Santa pinned a medal on Casey's jacket. The award said, "CHRISTMAS ELF OF THE YEAR"!

*C*asey was the happiest little elf in Santa Land that year. He puffed his chest out proudly as he wore the medal pinned to his jacket.

"Next year," said Cornelius, "Casey will be in charge of making all our dancing dolls."

Best of all, Mattie and her ballerina doll had the most special Christmas ever!

O Christmas

TREE

*J*enny said, "Just think. Tomorrow is Christmas Eve!" Jenny and Matt and Michelle were excited. Today they were going with their father to buy the Christmas tree.

"I know just what kind of tree we should have," said Jenny. "A tree tall enough to touch the ceiling. That would be perfect."

"No," said Matt. "Our tree should be big and wide. That's more important than tall."

"What I think," said Michelle, "is that it should be the most special tree ever!"

Mother smiled. "You're right about that, Michelle," she said. "We all want it to be the most special tree ever."

*T*hen Father said, "All right, let's get going!" Jenny and Matt and Michelle hurried to put on their coats and mittens, bundling up against the winter wind. It was a long way to the Christmas tree lot.

"Look in that store window," said Jenny when they got to town. "I see a toy shop with elves making toys."

"And I see Rudolph and the other reindeer in that one!" cried Matt.

Michelle looked, too, but she had other things on her mind. She was searching for the Christmas tree lot. It seemed to take forever to get there. But Father finally said, "Well, here we are." Michelle was the first to run over to the fence.

*J*enny quickly spotted the tree she wanted. She picked out a very tall, thin pine. "This is the one," she said.

But Matt said, "Here is a better one." He pointed to a short, wide tree with full branches.

None of the Christmas trees seemed right to Michelle. Then, in a corner of the lot, she saw a scraggly little tree that seemed to say, "Please pick me. I want to be your tree."

"Here is the one I want," called Michelle. The others came over.

At first they laughed at such a small tree, but finally Father said, "All right. If you insist, this is the one it will be."

When they got home, Mother was surprised to see such a small tree. "Michelle insisted," said Father with a smile, "so here it is."

Just then, Grandma and Grandpa arrived. "Now we can all decorate the tree together," said Matt.

Jenny made a special string out of beads she had been saving. She wound them around the tree's branches. Matt hung the special toy soldier ornament he had made at school. And Michelle put her angel doll at the very top.

Grandma said, "Your tree is a bit small, but you have made it look beautiful. I can see why you love it so. I think it's a special tree, too."

The next night, Christmas Eve, everyone gathered around the tree to sing:

O Christmas tree! O Christmas tree!
Your leaves are faithful ever!
O Christmas tree! O Christmas tree!
Your leaves are faithful ever!
Not only green when summer glows,
But in the winter when it snows,
O Christmas tree! O Christmas tree!
Your leaves are faithful ever!

As they sang, right before their eyes, the little tree became more and more beautiful. Lights twinkled from every branch, and its bright bulbs sparkled. The little tree seemed to be saying, "Look how beautiful I am, and how happy I am to be your Christmas tree!"

*T*he next morning was Christmas! When the family got up, the little tree was as beautiful as ever.

Santa had filled all their stockings and left presents under the tree. "Oh!" cried Jenny. "Look at this doll house. And it even has furniture inside!"

Matt said, "This train engine is great! I can't wait to try it out!"

And Michelle squealed, "What a beautiful doll Santa left for me! I think I'll name her Sally."

As it saw the happy children, the little tree seemed to smile and say, "I'm proud to be your special Christmas tree."

A week after Christmas, Grandma and Grandpa left. Then mother said, "It's time to take down our Christmas tree."

"I know what," said Michelle. "Let's plant our tree in the yard. That way we'll always have it. Maybe it will grow."

But Jenny and Matt laughed. "You can't plant a Christmas tree in a yard, silly," said Jenny.

"Can't we please just try?" begged Michelle.

"All right," said Father. "I know how much you children have loved our special little tree. We'll try. But don't expect it to work."

And so Father dug a hole, and they all held a little tree-planting ceremony.

*A*ll winter long, Michelle kept a special watch over her little tree. Every day, she looked out the window to see if the tree was still standing in the snow.

At first, Jenny and Matt smiled when they saw Michelle at the window. "Doesn't she know that a Christmas tree can't be planted?" Matt whispered to Jenny.

But before long, Jenny and Matt began to look out the window every day with Michelle.

"At first I thought your idea was silly," said Jenny. "But maybe it really will work."

"I know it will," said Michelle. "I think our little tree loved us as much as we loved it."

Spring finally came. On the first warm day, Jenny and Matt and Michelle went outdoors. Michelle ran to see their little tree.

She called, "Jenny, Matt, come look!" Jenny and Matt came running over. Sure enough, there were some bright green new branches growing from the tree.

"I *told* you our Christmas tree was special!" Michelle said. "I *knew* it would be here for us in the spring."

With that, Jenny and Matt and Michelle made a circle around the little tree and began to dance around it, singing, *"O Christmas Tree, O Christmas Tree, your branches green delight us."*

The little tree waved its new branches in the warm spring wind. It seemed to smile and say, "Thank you for being so kind to me. Now each time you look at me, you can remember Christmas. It will be like having the spirit of Christmas in your yard all year 'round!"

THE *Elves* AND THE
Shoemaker

*O*nce upon a time, long ago, there lived a shoemaker. He was an honest shoemaker and worked very hard. But no matter how hard he tried, he only got poorer and poorer. One day, he had nothing left but a bit of leather—just enough for a pair of shoes.

That night, before going to bed, he cut the leather into pieces. He would use the leather the next day to make his last pair of shoes. He laid the pieces carefully on his workbench.

"Tomorrow, I will wake up early and be ready to make my shoes," he said. Then he and his wife left the shop and went home to eat a small meal and go to bed.

The next morning, when the shoemaker and his wife returned to the shop, they found that the pieces of leather were no longer on the workbench. Instead, to their surprise and joy, there was a beautiful new pair of perfectly made shoes! The shoemaker looked at the shoes and found that they were much better than any he had ever made.

"Who could have done this?" wondered the shoemaker's wife.

In a short while, an elegant man entered the shop. He tried on the shoes and was so pleased that he offered a handsome price for them. The shoemaker took the money and bought enough leather for two pairs of shoes.

That night, the shoemaker again cut the leather for shoes to make the next day. He carefully laid the pieces out on his workbench. Then he went home.

And the next morning, when he and his wife returned to the shop, there were two pairs of shoes waiting on the workbench. These shoes were more beautiful than the ones they had found the day before.

Soon, a fine man and an elegant lady came into the shop. "What lovely shoes!" exclaimed the lady. She and the gentleman were so delighted that they paid an even higher price for the shoes than the man of the day before. Now the shoemaker was able to buy enough leather to make four pairs of shoes.

And so it went, night after night. The shoemaker would cut the leather for more and more shoes. He would carefully lay out the pieces, and each morning there would be rows of handsome shoes waiting on his workbench.

The word spread all around the countryside about the shoemaker's fine shoes. People began coming from far and wide to see for themselves and buy shoes at his shop.

Before long, the shoemaker and his wife were no longer poor. In fact, they were becoming very rich indeed. They had enough money to eat well and buy new clothes. They could hardly believe their good fortune!

*T*hen one evening, a few weeks before Christmas, the shoemaker said to his wife, "How I would like to know who is making such fine shoes for us! Let's stay awake tonight and find out."

"An excellent idea," said his wife. "I would love to know who has been helping us all these nights."

So the shoemaker and his wife went to the shop that very night. They took a candle and set it on a table near his workbench.

"We must hide ourselves," said the shoemaker. They crouched behind some clothes hanging in the corner of the room, and there they waited.

At the stroke of midnight, as the shoemaker and his wife watched, two little elves wearing thin and tattered clothes came into the shop. They immediately jumped onto the bench and began their work. How their fingers flew as they stitched and hammered and pounded away!

The shoemaker and his wife could hardly believe their eyes. The elves did not stop until all the leather was made into shoes.

When they had finished with their work, they swept up all the scraps of leather and left the workbench as they had found it. Then, in a twinkling, they jumped down and scurried out of the shop.

The next morning, the shoemaker's wife said, "Those two little elves have done so much for us. We should make a gift for them to show our thanks. They must be cold with their ragged clothes, so I will make two little suits and hats. Will you make two tiny pairs of boots for them?"

"Of course," said the shoemaker. So they set to work to make clothes for the elves.

The wife made two handsome coats of green wool. Then she sewed two tiny shirts of the finest cloth. She made two little hats and trimmed each one with a jaunty feather. She knitted two pairs of warm stockings. The shoemaker sewed two pairs of little boots. That night, they laid out their gifts on the workbench.

At midnight, sure enough, the two little elves came skipping into the shop, ready for work. They looked at the workbench, expecting to find pieces of leather to make into shoes.

But when they saw the beautiful tiny clothes, they were puzzled at first. Then their surprise turned to delight! They quickly began to dress themselves in the suits, shirts, little hats, and boots.

As they put on their clothes, they started to dance a lively jig. They hopped about and clapped their hands with glee. Then they began to sing:

Now we are jaunty gentlemen,
Why should we ever work again?

*A*s soon as they were dressed, they started dancing faster and faster. They hopped and laughed and sang until, at last, they twirled right out the door of the shop.

The shoemaker and his wife watched them dance down the snow-covered, moonlit path. The shoemaker smiled and said, "I wonder if we will ever see them again."

"Perhaps not," answered his wife. "But how glad I am we were able to repay them for all they have done for us. This is our happiest Christmas ever!"

The shoemaker and his wife never did see the two little elves again.

From that day on, though, the two of them had very good luck in all that they did. And they never forgot those who had helped them when they needed it most—the two little elves.

THE LITTLE

Drummer Boy

*A*long time ago, near the town of Bethlehem, there lived a little boy whose family was very poor. His clothes were not fancy. Sometimes he was hungry, for there was not enough food to eat.

But the boy had one thing that made his life happy. He had a drum. The drum had belonged to his father, and before that, to his grandfather. Years before, when his grandfather was young, a group of traveling musicians had come to the little village. His grandfather was given the drum by the musicians.

When the little boy was old enough, they taught him to play *pa-rum pum pum pum*. Now the drum belonged to him.

The little boy loved his drum more than anything in the world. In fact, he played his drum every day all around his village. The other children in the village would follow behind him, marching and singing along as he played. Sometimes, even the animals joined the parade!

The boy played his drum so often and so well that the people in the village began to call him the Little Drummer Boy. They always smiled as they heard him playing and singing:

Pa-rum pum pum pum,
Me and my drum.

At the same time, in a town called Nazareth, there lived a young girl named Mary. One day, the Angel Gabriel appeared to Mary and told her that she would have a son and should name the baby Jesus.

Now, Caesar Augustus, who was the ruler of the land, sent out an order. All the people had to go to the town where they were born. There, the tax collectors would count them and write down their names.

So Mary and her husband, Joseph, set out on the long journey from Nazareth to Bethlehem. They had to travel slowly, because Mary was expecting a baby. Mary rode on a donkey, and Joseph walked along beside her.

When Mary and Joseph finally arrived in Bethlehem, it was crowded with all the people who had come to be counted. Joseph asked at many houses for a place to spend the night, but no one had room for them. Night was coming, and it was growing cold outside.

Finally, Joseph and Mary came to an inn. They again asked for a room. The innkeeper said, "I have no room inside, but there is a stable behind the inn where you could stay with the animals tonight."

Mary and Joseph were so cold and tired they were happy to have any place to spend the night. So they went to the little stable and slept on the hay with the animals.

During the night, the baby was born. It was a boy, just as the Angel Gabriel had said. Mary named the baby Jesus and wrapped him in swaddling clothes. She made a bed for him by putting hay in a manger. Then she carefully laid him on the hay.

That same night, some shepherds were in a nearby field watching over their sheep. All of a sudden, an angel appeared to them and told them about the birth of Jesus.

The angel said, "Go to Bethlehem, where you will find the newborn baby, lying in a manger." Then many angels appeared and sang, "Peace on earth and good will to all." When the angels disappeared, the shepherds hurried to the manger where the baby Jesus lay.

*E*veryone was talking about baby Jesus and wanted to take gifts to him. The Little Drummer Boy heard this and thought, "I want to go to see Jesus, too. But what can I take as a present?"

That night, when he started to Bethlehem, he saw a magnificent sight. In front of him were three kings, their camels laden with heavy saddlebags. The kings were dressed in the finest clothes the boy had ever seen. Were they also going to see the baby Jesus?

The Little Drummer Boy listened as he followed them. "There is the star we follow," said one. "That bright and shining star has led us over many lands for many nights. See, it points us toward the stable ahead."

*T*he three kings followed the star to the manger where the baby Jesus lay. When the kings arrived, all the people who had gathered around stood back. "Who are you?" asked a shepherd.

"My name is Melchior," said the first, "and I have brought a gift of gold for the newborn baby."

The second said, "I am Gaspar. I have brought frankincense, a rare and beautiful perfume."

"And my name is Balthazar," said the third. "I, too, have brought a valuable perfume, called myrrh."

The three kings laid their gifts before the manger and said, "We have followed the star for many miles to see the newborn baby."

The Little Drummer Boy saw the beautiful gifts the kings had brought. "Oh, what can I do?" he thought. "I have nothing to give!" He hung his head and began to walk away.

Then he saw the drum at his side. Suddenly he knew what his gift could be. He would sing and play his drum for the baby Jesus!

Come, they told me, pa-rum pum pum pum,
Our newborn King to see, pa-rum pum pum pum.
Our finest gifts we bring, pa-rum pum pum pum
To lay before the King, pa-rum pum pum pum
Rum pum pum pum, rum pum pum pum,
So to honor Him, pa-rum pum pum pum,
When we come.